THE PARTY'S ABOUT TO START AND YOU'RE INVITED!

stardoll™

Secrets & Dreams

JAYJAY JACKSON – Writer & Artist

NEW YORK

STARDOLL is a virtual paper doll community site for everyone who enjoys fame, fashion and friends – and the inspiration for this series of graphic novels by JayJay Jackson. At stardoll.com you can create your own MeDoll or choose from an ever-growing collection of celebrity dolls and dress them up in a wide selection of fashions. Every celebrity doll has a wardrobe full of unique clothes and there are new dolls released every week. The non-superstar membership is free.

Stardoll's original name was Paperdollheaven.com, and started out as the hobby of the Scandinavian-born Liisa. Inspired by a childhood passion for paper dolls, Liisa started drawing dolls and accompanying wardrobes and taught herself web design. Her personal homepage rapidly became a popular destination for teens. In 2004, with the help of her son, she upgraded the site and called it Paperdoll Heaven.

Stardoll is one of few places on the Internet developed with an emphasis on girls' self-expression through fantasy and fashion play. Stardoll.com is a great place to spend time with friends and to meet other kids from all over the world. It's an inspiring, safe and creative environment. "Most online sites are focused on violence and competitiveness," says Liisa. "I wanted to create a positive online environment for young girls who are creative and interested in fashion. They are looking for alternatives to shoot 'em up and kill 'em games." Liisa is still an important part of the Stardoll family and she makes new paper dolls every week.

STARDOLL
#1 "Secrets & Dreams"
JayJay Jackson – Writer, Artist, Colorist, Letterer
Special thanks to Jim Shooter, James Fry and Joe James for all of their help!
And thank you to Ashley Skeels, Ruby Claire Roessler, Trish Aponte, and Sue-Ni DiStefano.
JayJay Jackson – Design & Production
Beth Scorzato – Production Coordinator
Associate Editor – Michael Petranek
Jim Salicrup
Editor-in-Chief

ISBN: 978-1-59707-418-6 paperback edition
ISBN: 978-1-59707-419-3 hardcover edition

Printed in Canada
July 2013 by Friesens Printing
1 Printers Way
Altona, MB ROG OBO

Papercutz books may be purchased for business or promotional use.
For information on bulk purchases please contact Macmillan Corporate
and Premium Sales Department at (800) 221-7945 x5442.

Distributed by Macmillan
First Printing

Los Angeles High School of Fashion and Design

Student information sheet

Name: Ashley Archer

Eye Color: Brown

Hair Color: Dark Blonde

Fashion Style: Feminine, Athletic

Goals: Fashion business management

Interests: Parkour, Capoeira, Extreme Sports

Other: "Always do what is right. It will gratify half of mankind and astound the other." - Mark Twain

Los Angeles High School of Fashion and Design

Student information sheet

Name: Claire Leo

Eye Color: Blue

Hair Color: Deep Auburn

Fashion Style: Casual, Fashion Forward

Goals: Fashion designer

Interests: Drawing, Sewing, Pattern making

Other: I have two cats. Their names are Chloé and Chanel

Los Angeles High School of Fashion and Design

Student information sheet

Name: *Kaya Reynard*

Eye Color: *Gold*

Hair Color: *Rich Bright Auburn*

Fashion Style: *Eclectic, Urban*

Goals: *Interior Designer*

Interests: *Family and friends, socializing*

Other: *I love to create look books out of fashion magazines.*

Los Angeles High School of Fashion and Design

Student information sheet

Name: Ruby Zara

Eye Color: Grey

Hair Color: Changeable

Fashion Style: 80s Vintage, Geek Chic

Goals: Fashion Technology

Interests: Internet, Technology,
Cultural Studies

Other: My Faves: Dancing to 80s music,
watching John Hughes movies.

Los Angeles High School of Fashion and Design

Student information sheet

Name: *Sue-Ni MacDuffie*

Eye Color: *Aquamarine*

Hair Color: *Black with an aqua streak*

Fashion Style: *Pretty, Asian inspired*

Goals: *Fashion Buyer*

Interests: *Bollywood Dance, Swimming, Shopping*

Other: *Guilty pleasures: Romance novels and Bollywood musicals*

HOLD STILL A SEC. I JUST WANT TO MAKE SURE THIS DRAPES RIGHT.
NEXT UP ON THE RUNWAY ARE THE SOPHOMORE CLASS FASHIONS...
STARTING WITH FIVE OUTFITS BY NEWCOMER, *CLAIRE LEO.*
EEEEEEEEEEEEEEEEEEEEEEEEEEEEEEEK!

YooScreen

Search

Kallenation, Episode 28, Season Finale

Upload

Sign In

Log Out

Playlist

Settings

Media

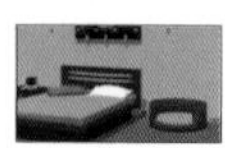

Kallenation Episode 1

Kallenation Episode 2

Kallenation Episode 3

GIRLS, YOUR FATHER HAS SOMETHING *VERY* IMPORTANT TO TELL YOU.
YOU KNOW I'VE BEEN WORKING A LOT LATELY AND HAVEN'T BEEN ABLE TO BE HOME MUCH, BUT TODAY THE I.P.O. ON MY DOT-COM EXCEEDED ALL EXPECTATIONS AND CLOSED AT TRIPLE THE OFFERING PRICE.

HUH?

I MEAN TO SAY...
WE'RE RICH!
THESE PRESENTS ARE FOR *YOU!*
NOW, LET'S GO *HOUSE HUNTING!*
Extreme Doll House
SEW 5000

WE'RE *MOVING?*
WHAT ABOUT MY *FRIENDS?* AND MY BEST FRIEND, *VIV?*
YOU EACH GET YOUR *OWN ROOM!*
AND YOU CAN STILL SEE VIV ON WEEKENDS!
AND, CLAIRE, *NOW* YOU'LL BE ABLE TO APPLY TO FASHION SCHOOL! IT'S WHAT YOU'VE *DREAMED* ABOUT!

A BUSY COUPLE OF MONTHS LATER, AT THE NEW HOUSE IN A FASHIONABLE SECTION OF LA...
CLAIRE'S ROOM
CLAIRE'S ROOM
WHAT A **NIGHTMARE!** MY **FIRST** DAY AS A SOPHOMORE AT THE FASHION HIGH SCHOOL OF MY DREAMS...
AND I HAVE **NO** IDEA WHAT TO WEAR!

TODAY'S OUTFIT IS **MAKE OR BREAK!**

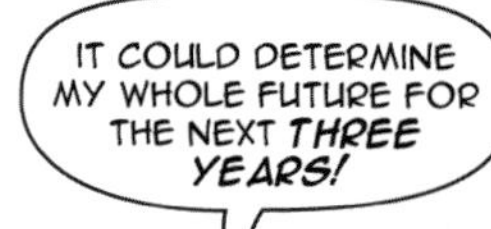
IT COULD DETERMINE MY WHOLE FUTURE FOR THE NEXT **THREE YEARS!**

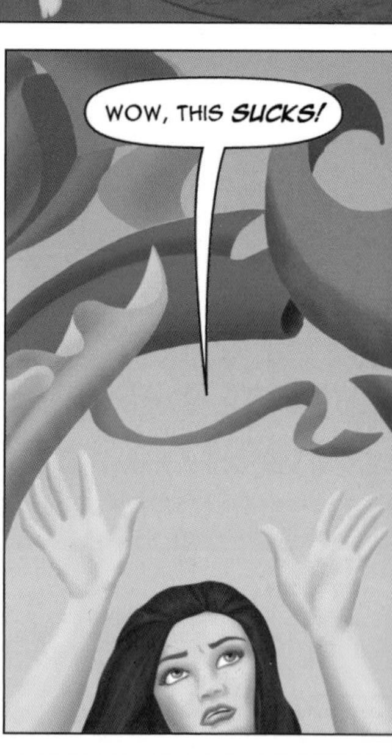
WOW, THIS **SUCKS!**

CLAIRE!
IF WE DON'T LEAVE **RIGHT NOW** YOU'LL BE LATE!

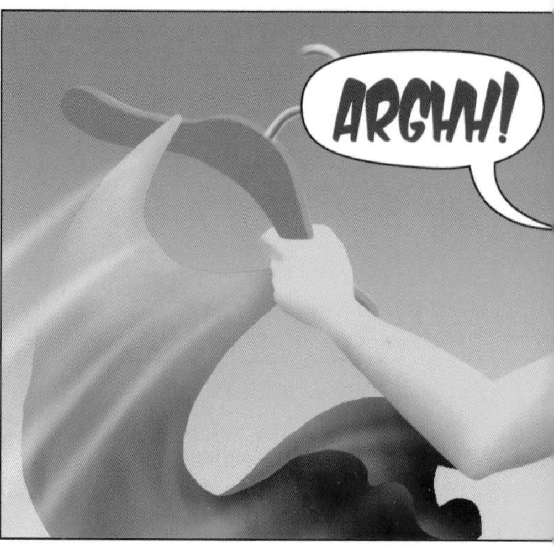
ARGHH!

Los Angeles High School
of Fashion and Design

ME.

CUTE BAG! IS THAT A KATELYN?
YES, IT IS! YOU LIKE KATELYN, TOO?

I LOVE HER STUFF! HI, I'M CLAIRE.
I'M ASHLEY. NICE SHOES!
THANKS!

CAN YOU POINT ME TOWARD THE OFFICE? I NEED TO PICK UP MY SCHEDULE.
NEW TO *FAD?*
FAD?

FASHION AND DESIGN. *FAD.*
RIGHT. GOT IT. YEP, I'M A NOOB.

YOU'LL LIKE IT. IT'S A PRETTY TOUGH SCHOOL, BUT IN A GOOD WAY.

HERE'S THE OFFICE. MEET ME IN THE CAFETERIA AT LUNCH TIME AND I'LL INTRODUCE YOU AROUND. WE SIT BY THE *MARSHMALLOWS.*

THE *MARSHMALLOWS?*
YOU'LL SEE.

CLAIRE!
OVER HERE!

HI THERE! EVERYBODY, THIS IS **CLAIRE.**
MARSHMALLOWS. NOW I GET IT. CUTE CHAIRS.

EVERYTHING IS DESIGN-Y AT FAD.
SEEMS **FUN.**
IT'S INSPIRING.

INTRODUCTIONS... THIS IS KAYA, SHE'S INTO WORLD BEAUTIFICATION.
INTERIOR DESIGN.
RUBY, SHE'S A TECH-HEAD.
FASHION TECHNOLOGIES AND INNOVATION. IT'S AWESOME.
AND SUE-NI WANTS TO SHOP FOR A LIVING.
I'M STUDYING TO BE A FASHION BUYER. I ALREADY HAVE AN INTERNSHIP AT BARNEY'S LINED UP FOR SENIOR YEAR.
CLAIRE WANTS TO BE A FASHION DESIGNER. MAYBE SHE'LL MAKE OUR PROM DRESSES IF WE'RE NICE.
I DO HAVE SOME EXPERIENCE WITH THAT.
AND I'M INTERESTED IN THE BUSINESS SIDE OF FASHION. I WANT TO DISCOVER NEW TALENT.

SO... CLAIRE DO YOU HAVE A SKETCHBOOK?
ALWAYS! HERE.
SKETCHBOOK

DID ANYONE SEE THE NEW YORK FASHION WEEK SHOWS LAST NIGHT?
SURE. THAT OTHERWORLD RUNWAY SHOW WAS OUTRAGEOUS!
APPARENTLY HE THINKS METAL IS THE NEW BLACK.
SKETCHBOOK

THESE ARE REALLY GOOD!
I BELIEVE YOU MAY HAVE A FUTURE. YOU'RE GOING TO DO WELL HERE.
THANKS!

WE'RE GOING SHOPPING AFTER SCHOOL. WANT TO COME?
REALLY? WHERE DO YOU GUYS USUALLY GO?

WE LIKE MELROSE FOR EDGY, SUNSET FOR FASHION VICTIM, ABBOT KINNEY FOR VINTAGE AND RODEO FOR RESEARCH. BUT TODAY WE'RE HEADED TO THE STARPLAZA.
THAT'S PRETTY FAR. HOW DO YOU GET THERE?
KAYA'S BROTHER WILL DRIVE US. HE USUALLY OWES HER A FAVOR FOR SOMETHING.
USUALLY? TRY ALWAYS. I KEEP HIM OUT OF TROUBLE, SO IT'S THE LEAST HE CAN DO.

HI, GAL PALS! YOU TOO, KAYA.
OH, GEORGIANA, YOU HERE AGAIN? HI, OLIVIA.
HEY.

NICE RIPPED PANTS, KAYA. FASHION ROADKILL SUITS YOU.
NICE TOP, GEORGIANA. COVERING A SUDDEN WEIGHT GAIN?

I FORGOT TO GET KETCHUP. OLIVIA, YOU'RE SO SWEET, WOULD YOU MIND GETTING SOME FOR ME?
OH, SURE. NEXT TIME I'M OVER THERE. LIKE MAYBE TOMORROW.

HEY GUYS. HI, RUBY.
AJAY, WOULD YOU MIND FETCHING ME SOME KETCHUP? PRETTY PLEASE?
WE HAVE CLASS. SEE YOU LATER.

AJAY, IF YOU DO I WILL BREAK YOUR SHIN WITH A MARSHMALLOW.

AJAY?
UH-UH. SHE SCARES ME.

FINE! I'LL GET IT MYSELF.
IT BUILDS CHARACTER.

THANKS FOR INTRODUCING ME TO YOUR FRIENDS, ASHLEY. THIS IS TURNING OUT TO BE A PRETTY GOOD FIRST DAY OF SCHOOL!
MEET US OUT IN FRONT AFTER SCHOOL AND WE'LL GO TO THE MALL.
SURE!
YOU GUYS ARE FUN TO HANG OUT WITH!
LATERS!

LATERS...AT THE MALL...
SUE-NI, ARE YOU GETTING THAT OMBRE INFINITY SCARF?
IT'S SO SWEET! BUT I LOVE THESE PINK TEASHADES. I CAN'T DECIDE.

I REALLY THINK I NEED THIS TANGERINE CLUTCH AND MATCHING WIDE BELT.
I DON'T HAVE ENOUGH TANGERINE IN MY WARDROBE. I'M ORANGE DEFICIENT.

KAYA, WHAT DO YOU THINK? I'M CONSIDERING LIMITING MY WARDROBE TO THREE COLORS. STREAMLINING! VERY PRACTICAL.
I DON'T KNOW, RUBY, HOW COULD YOU EVER PICK JUST THREE COLORS?

I'M THINKING EIGHTIES THEME. AQUA, MAGENTA AND BLACK.
A BOLDLY ANTI-TRENDY MOVE! I FORESEE MUCH VINTAGE SHOPPING IN YOUR FUTURE.
I LIKE RETRO STYLE, BUT I WANT MY RETRO TO BE NEW.

I CAN'T AFFORD ANYTHING. MY DAD TOTALLY REFUSED TO GIVE ME A CREDIT CARD. HE SAYS HE WANTS ME TO REMEMBER WHERE I CAME FROM.
CASE OF THE "ROOTS," HUH?
OH, YEAH.
YOU SHOULD TELL HIM YOU NEED IT FOR SCHOOL. HE WOULDN'T KNOW WHAT YOU NEED FOR SUPPLIES, FABRICS AND STUFF. PLUS ALL THE FASHION RESEARCH... MAGAZINES, BOOKS.
THAT'S A GREAT IDEA. YOU KNOW, YOU'RE PRETTY DEVIOUS.
I'M A TEENAGER.
MY BROTHER, KALLEN, AND HIS FRIEND, SEBASTIAN, ARE ON THEIR WAY. THEY'VE BEEN WORKING ON SOME TOP SECRET PROJECT. SO YOU KNOW THAT'S GOING TO BE TROUBLE. AS USUAL.
HEY, HEY, EVERYBODY! YOU ARE ALL CHOSEN TO STAR IN THE PREMIERE EPISODE OF KALLENATION! NO AUTOGRAPHS, PLEASE.
THE CROWD GOES WILD!
SEBASTIAN, STOP FILMING! WHAT THE HECK ARE YOU TWO DOING?

WE'RE MAKING OUR OWN REALTY SHOW! AND YOU GUYS ARE IN IT!
DON'T YOU GET ENOUGH OF THAT STUFF? IT'S ALL YOU EVER WATCH!
I'M NOT DRESSED FOR BEING FILMED!
NONE OF US HAVE OUR MAKEUP DONE!

I'VE DECIDED THAT'S WHAT I WANT TO BE! A REALITY TV STAR. I AUDITIONED BUT THEY NEVER CALLED, SO I'M TIRED OF WAITING. WE'RE GOING TO DO IT OURSELVES.
WE GOT OUR OWN YOOSCREEN CHANNEL!

ARE YOU KIDDING ME?
YOU CAN'T DO THIS.
OH, WHAT ARE YOU SO WORRIED ABOUT? C'MON, SEBASTIAN, LETS FILM THE INTRODUCTIONS.

THIS IS MY BEAUTIFUL SISTER, KAYA... WELL, MOST OF THE TIME SHE'S BEAUTIFUL. NOT RIGHT NOW.
KALLEN! CUT IT OUT!

AND THESE ARE HER FRIENDS...
UH...
I'M NOT TOO SURE THIS IS A GOOD IDEA.
I'M PRETTY SURE IT'S NOT. YOU DIDN'T ASK US IF WE WANTED TO BE IN IT. ARE YOU EVEN GETTING MODEL RELEASES?
IT SOUNDS KIND OF FUN. WHAT'S THE SHOW GOING TO BE ABOUT?

WELL, HEY THERE. ARE WE MAKING A MOVIE?
WE ARE CREATING A REALITY SHOW, GEORGIANA, MY SISTER'S FRIEND.

CAN I BE IN IT?
YOU ALREADY ARE!

IT'S GOING TO BE RAW. REAL!

GUERILLA FILMMAK--
ACK!
WE'RE GOING HOME!
NOW!

WHAT COULD YOU BE THINKING?!

OF ALL OF THE BONEHEAD THINGS YOU'VE DONE THIS IS THE BONEHEADIEST! YOU HAVE TO STOP NOW!
NO WAY! EVER SINCE GRADUATION I'VE BEEN TRYING TO FIGURE OUT WHAT TO DO WITH MY LIFE AND THIS IS IT! I WOULD BE GREAT AT BEING FAMOUS!

YOU CAN'T BE FAMOUS. NONE OF OUR KIND CAN BE FAMOUS! THAT WOULD ENDANGER US ALL. YOU KNOW THAT!
NO, I DON'T "KNOW" THAT. IT'S RIDICULOUS, ANYWAY. HOW WOULD ANYONE FIND OUT ABOUT US?

WE ALWAYS HAVE TO BE SO CAREFUL, FIT IN, NEVER CALL ATTENTION TO OURSELVES... WHY?
WELL, I CALL BULLHOCKEY. I WASN'T MADE TO "FIT IN!" THIS IS MY DREAM. AND I CAN HANDLE IT. WHY DON'T YOU EVER TRUST ME?

TRUST YOU?! YOU SELFISH JERK! YOU'D RISK EVERYTHING, ALL OF OUR LIVES... YOU DON'T HAVE THE RIGHT TO DO THAT!

YOU--!

IF MOM AND DAD FIND OUT YOU'LL BE GROUNDED UNTIL YOU'RE DEAD!

Yoo Screen
Search
Kallenation, Episode 1
Upload
Sign In
Log Out
Playlist
Settings
Media
24 Views
No Comments

Kallenation
Episode 2

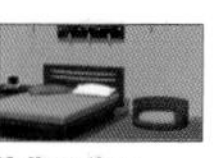
Kallenation
Episode 3

Kallenation
Episode 4

Kallenation
Episode 5

THE SHOW JUST LACKS *DRAMA*. THAT'S WHAT IS SO GREAT ABOUT REALITY SHOWS... ***THE FIGHTING!***
WE'LL JUST FILM YOU AND YOUR SISTER, THEN. PLENTY OF FIGHTING.

WE NEED PLOTS, SUBPLOTS, CRAZY CHARACTERS. ***GIRLS!*** WE NEED IT TO BUILD UP TO A GIANT ***DRAMA BOMB***.
A CRAZY ***DRAMACOASTER!***
A ***DRAMACANO!***

YEAH, BUT ***HOW?***
LET'S GO TALK TO MY SISTER'S FRIENDS...

... SO I WANT TO GET EVERYONE TOGETHER AT OUR HOUSE AND SHOWCASE EVERYONE'S *TALENTS.*

DOES *KAYA* KNOW ABOUT THIS?
I ONLY JUST HAD THE IDEA TODAY. BUT SHE'LL BE OKAY WITH IT. WHY *WOULDN'T* SHE?

I'D BE TOO EMBARRASSED TO HAVE SO MANY PEOPLE WATCHING ME.
YEAH... WELL, WE HAVE HARDLY ANY VIEWERS. SO, THAT'S *NOT* REALLY A PROBLEM.

I DON'T REALLY *HAVE* ANY TALENTS.
THIS IS THE PERFECT OPPORTUNITY TO *DISCOVER* SOME!

I THINK IT SOUNDS LIKE *FUN*. WHEN ARE YOU PLANNING TO DO THIS?
TOMORROW'S SATURDAY! ARE YOU GUYS FREE?

WAS THAT MY *BROTHER?*

I HOPE YOU KNOW WHAT YOU'RE DOING.
IT'LL BE **FINE.** YOU WORRY TOO MUCH.

YOU **NEVER** WORRY. **SOMEONE** HAS TO.

SO, THIS WILL BE **GREAT!** RUBY WILL HELP SEBASTIAN WITH THE FILMING...

"CLAIRE WILL DO FASHION MAKEOVERS..."
ORANGE WILL ENHANCE YOUR SKIN COLOR AND BRING OUT YOUR EYES!

SUE-NI WILL DO BOLLYWOOD DANCE.
ASHLEY WILL DEMONSTRATE BRAZILIAN DANCE FIGHTING, CAPOEIRA.
HEY, IS THIS THE PARTY?
KALLEN! YOU INVITED GEORGIANA?

Search

Upload

Kallenation, Episode 14

Sign In

Log Out

Playlist

Settings

Media

482 Views

42 Comments

Kallenation Episode 1

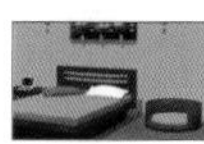

Kallenation Episode 2

Kallenation Episode 3

Kallenation Episode 4

42 Comments

Skeeterdude

Your show is better with the girls, especially Georgiana. She's fierce. More Georgiana!

AnnMarie9700

I noticed all of the rooms in your house have dog beds. Where is your dog?

Reply

KallenReyn

He ran away. Sad.

★L.A.H.S. OF FASHION & DESIGN★
CALL FOR ENTRIES!
FALL FASHION SHOW
DEADLINE FOR DESIGNS-1 WEEK
HEY DESIGNERS! LOOK!
SUBMIT 6 DESIGNS MINIMUM
DREAM A DREAM OF STYLE
★ SUBMIT DESIGNS TO MRS BARTEAU, ROOM 242 ★
FOR MORE INFO SEE WWW.LAHSFAD.ORG/FALLFASHION
CLAIRE, YOU ***HAVE*** TO GO FOR IT!
YOU'LL GET IN FOR ***SURE!***
YOU REALLY THINK SO?
ABSOLUTELY! YOUR DESIGNS ARE ***AMAZING!***
BESIDES, WE CAN HELP YOU MA
THE OUTFITS!

THIS IS A *LOT* HARDER THAN I IMAGINED.
I'M WRACKING MY BRAIN FOR EVERY OUNCE OF CREATIVITY.
I'VE BEEN WORKING EVERY NIGHT UNTIL I FALL ASLEEP, EXHAUSTED.
I LOVE IT!

NEXT WEEK...
Claire Leo Fashion Show Submission
APPROVED

I **KNEW** YOU'D GET IN!

THESE ARE SO BEAUTIFUL! I WANT TO MODEL ***THIS ONE!***
Claire Leo Fashion Show Submission
APPROVED

I MIGHT HAVE SOME IDEAS ABOUT ***NEW MATERIALS.***

TIME TO GO ***SHOPPING!***

SOON, AT CLAIRE'S HOUSE, THE GIRLS ARE HARD AT WORK...
I CAME UP WITH THIS MATERIAL THAT ALWAYS SPRINGS BACK INTO SHAPE NO MATTER HOW YOU BEND IT. THINK YOU CAN USE IT?
DEFINITELY! IT WOULD BE PERFECT TO SHAPE A HIGH COLLAR.
YOU COULD EVEN MAKE SOME OF IT SWIRL AROUND THIS DRESS.
NICE! NO MORE IRONING OR STEAMING!
THAT TICKLES!
IS THERE ANY MORE OF THIS BLUE RIBBON?

KALLEN AND SEBASTIAN WANT TO COME OVER AND FILM US.
THAT MIGHT BE FUN.

IS EVERYONE **OKAY** WITH IT?
SURE.
YEP.
OKAY.
MMMHMM.

WE'VE BEEN GETTING MORE VIEWS ON YOOSCREEN LATELY, BUT MOST OF THE COMMENTS ARE FROM PEOPLE ASKING ABOUT THE ***EMPTY DOG BEDS.***
IT SEEMS LIKE THAT'S ***ALL*** ANYONE IS WATCHING OUR SHOW FOR.
YOU SAID YOUR DOG RAN AWAY? WHAT'S HIS NAME?

UM... *FUZZY.*
YOU MUST ***REALLY*** LOVE FUZZY. THOSE ARE BEAUTIFUL DOG BEDS. THEY LOOK SO ***COMFORTABLE!***

WHAT KIND OF DOG IS HE?
JUST A **REGULAR** DOG.
YOU POSTED A PICTURE OF HIM IN THE YOUSCREEN COMMENTS, RIGHT?

OH, **REALLY?** I DIDN'T KNOW WE **HAD** ANY PICTURES OF **FUZZY**.
!
WELL, IT **WAS** KIND OF... UM, FUZZY.

HAVEN'T YOU TRIED TO **FIND** HIM?

OH, **SURE...** BUT WE COULDN'T.
HEY! WHAT DO YOU CALL THAT COLOR?
I CALL IT **ADVENTURINE.** HOW LONG HAS FUZZY--?

HEY! YOU KNOW, WHAT WE NEED IS SOMETHING TO TAKE THE VIEWERS' MINDS OFF OF THE DOG.
MAYBE YOU GIRLS COULD GET INTO A BIG BRAWL. THAT ALWAYS RATES SUPER HIGH ON TV REALITY SHOWS!

WHAT?
SURE! YOU COULD ALL START ARGUING AND YELLING... A LITTLE HAIR-PULLING WOULD NOT BE TERRIBLE FOR OUR POPULARITY.

I THINK THAT WOULD BE PRETTY TERRIBLE.
SO DO I.

YOU GUYS... OUT!
BUT...

OUT! NOW!
GEEZ. BOSSY.

Kallenation, Episode 19
Upload
Sign In
Log Out
Playlist
Settings
Media

Kallenation
Episode 1

Kallenation
Episode 2

Kallenation
Episode 3

2,678 Views

NEXT WEEKEND.
HEY, CLAIRE, A LOT OF THESE COMMENTS ARE ABOUT YOUR DESIGNS FOR THE FASHION SHOW! PEOPLE ARE LOVING THEM!
WOW! NOW IF I CAN ONLY GET THE OUTFITS FINISHED IN TIME! I CALLED MY FRIEND VIV TO ASK HER TO HELP BUT SHE'S OUT OF THE COUNTRY WITH HER DAD.
THERE'S A LOT LEFT TO DO. WE REALLY COULD USE SOME HELP.
GEORGIANA IS A PRETTY GOOD SEAMSTRESS.
NO. OH, NO! NOT GEORGIANA!

IF WE DON'T GET SOME HELP, WE MAY NOT GET FINISHED. AND THERE'S EVEN THAT EXTRA DRESS THAT GEORGIANA COULD MODEL IF WE CAN GET IT DONE.

ARGHH! TALK ABOUT SUFFERING FOR ART! WHY ME?

YOU CAN **STOP** WORRYING GIRLS! **GEORGIANA'S** HERE NOW!
KALLEN, WHAT ARE **YOU** DOING HERE?

KAYA, YOU **MUST** LET THE SHOW GO ON! IT'S YOUR BROTHER'S **DREAM!**
I'LL BE GOOD! **PROMISE!**

NO MORE ACTING LIKE A JERK!
I'LL BE BETTER THAN GOOD! I'LL BE GREAT!

A BIT LATER...
WOW, GEORGIANA, YOU'RE FINISHED SEWING THAT DRESS **ALREADY?**
AND YOU EVEN DID **FRENCH SEAMS!**

I TOLD YOU SHE WAS GOOD.

KAYA, DEAR, YOUR HEM IS A BIT CROOKED. IT'S A BIAS CUT SKIRT, YOU HAVE TO HEM IT A LITTLE DIFFERENTLY. HERE, LET ME SHOW YOU.

GRRR.

PEOPLE KEEP ASKING ABOUT THE DOG IN ALL THE COMMENTS. SOME OF THEM HAVE EVEN SAID THEY WANT TO HELP US FIND IT.
ISN'T THAT A GOOD THING, TOO? SEEMS LIKE YOU MUST MISS HIM.
HMM... HEY, LOOK AT THIS COMMENT, CLAIRE...
WHAT'S IT SAY?
SOMEONE WHO SAYS HE'S A FASHION DESIGNER COMMENTED ABOUT YOUR DESIGNS.
WHAT?!
OH, HERE... LOOK AT THE GUY'S PROFILE. HE'S A FASHION DESIGNER IN MILAN. HIS CHANNEL SHOWS A BUNCH OF HIS FASHION SHOW VIDEOS.
WHOA. HE SAYS HE'S LOOKING FORWARD TO SEEING MY DESIGNS ON THE RUNWAY.

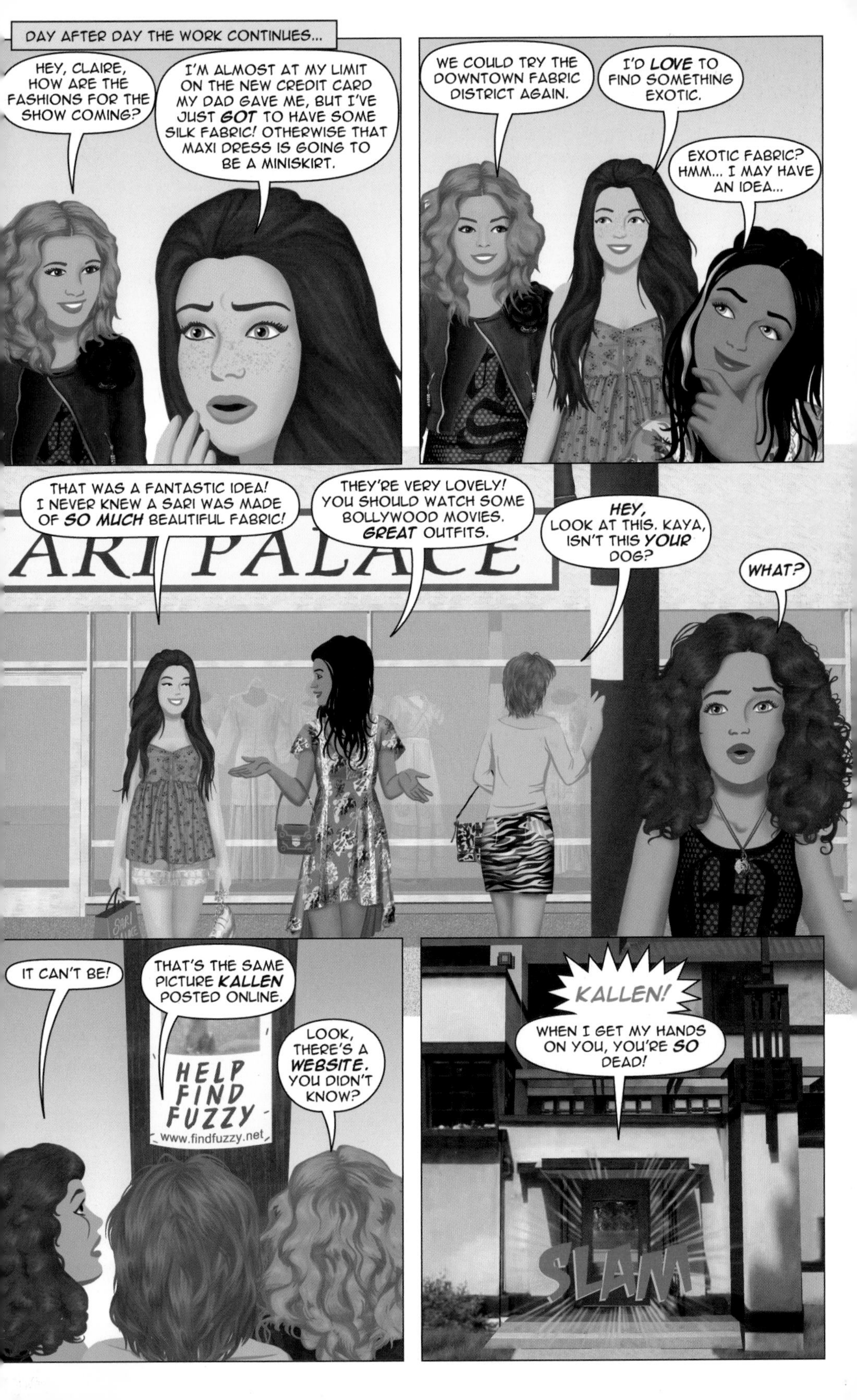
DAY AFTER DAY THE WORK CONTINUES...
HEY, CLAIRE, HOW ARE THE FASHIONS FOR THE SHOW COMING?
I'M ALMOST AT MY LIMIT ON THE NEW CREDIT CARD MY DAD GAVE ME, BUT I'VE JUST GOT TO HAVE SOME SILK FABRIC! OTHERWISE THAT MAXI DRESS IS GOING TO BE A MINISKIRT.
WE COULD TRY THE DOWNTOWN FABRIC DISTRICT AGAIN.
I'D LOVE TO FIND SOMETHING EXOTIC.
EXOTIC FABRIC? HMM... I MAY HAVE AN IDEA...
ARI PALACE
THAT WAS A FANTASTIC IDEA! I NEVER KNEW A SARI WAS MADE OF SO MUCH BEAUTIFUL FABRIC!
THEY'RE VERY LOVELY! YOU SHOULD WATCH SOME BOLLYWOOD MOVIES. GREAT OUTFITS.
HEY, LOOK AT THIS. KAYA, ISN'T THIS YOUR DOG?
WHAT?
IT CAN'T BE!
THAT'S THE SAME PICTURE KALLEN POSTED ONLINE.
HELP FIND FUZZY
www.findfuzzy.net
LOOK, THERE'S A WEBSITE. YOU DIDN'T KNOW?
KALLEN!
WHEN I GET MY HANDS ON YOU, YOU'RE SO DEAD!
SLAM

NEXT SATURDAY MORNING.
KALLEN, GET UP! YOU'RE DRIVING ME AND THE GIRLS TO BUY NOTIONS! WE'RE WORKING AT CLAIRE'S HOUSE AGAIN TODAY TO TRY AND GET FINISHED IN TIME FOR THE FASHION SHOW.
YIP!
JUST GET CHANGED! AND GET DRESSED.
MMRRFFF.
C'MON, JUST LET US COME AND FILM YOU GUYS WORKING TODAY. THE VIEWERS ARE REALLY INTERESTED IN THE PREPARATIONS FOR THE FASHION SHOW.
THEY'RE A LOT MORE INTERESTED IN HOW GORGEOUS GEORGIANA IS. AND IN THE "MISSING DOG." WHAT ARE YOU GOING TO DO ABOUT THAT?
IT'S NOTHING. THE "DOG" WON'T BE FOUND AND IT WILL JUST BLOW OVER.
KALLEN, THERE'S A "FIND FUZZY" WEBSITE AND A FACEBOOK PAGE. IT'S NOT BLOWING OVER. DON'T YOU CARE ABOUT ANYONE BUT YOURSELF?
CAN WE FILM OR NOT?
IF THE OTHER GIRLS SAY ITS OKAY.

THIS CORDING WOULD BE **PERFECT** IF IT WAS GOLD.
I FOUND THE GROMMETS YOU WANTED. AND SOME CUTE TRIM.
OOH! THAT **IS** CUTE!

THOSE BLACK PANTS JUST NEED **SOMETHING.**
HOW ABOUT CONCHOS?
THIS BLACK CHAIN HAS A CERTAIN *JE NE SAIS QUOI.* BUT I DON'T KNOW WHAT IT **IS.**

I LIKE CONCHOS, BUT THAT CHAIN LOOKS LIKE THE PERFECT THING. I'M PICTURING EDGY AND A LITTLE DANGEROUS.
BAD PANTS!

EVER NOTICE JUST HOW **GOOD** SHOPPING BAGS FEEL IN YOUR HANDS?
IT'S THE FEEL OF FRESH ACQUISITION.

SO, AFTER YOU DROP US OFF, CAN YOU PICK UP OLIVIA AND GEORGIANA AT HER HOUSE? THEY SAID THEY WOULD HELP OUT TODAY.
SURE.

AT THE LEO HOUSE...
KALLEN SHOULD BE BACK WITH OLIVIA AND GEORGIANA PRETTY SOON. SO, I HAVE TO ASK YOU GUYS... HE AND SEBASTIAN WANT TO COME AND FILM US AGAIN TODAY.

IT'S OKAY WITH ME. PEOPLE HAVE BEEN SAYING SUCH NICE THINGS ABOUT MY DESIGNS IN THE COMMENTS ON YOOSCREEN.
WHAT ABOUT YOU GUYS?

UM..
WELL...

I THINK WITH THE SHOW GETTING MORE ATTENTION, IT'S MORE...
...PRESSURE.
...EMBARRASSING.

OKAY. I'LL JUST TELL HIM IT'S A NO.
WHAT'S WRONG WITH YOU GUYS? KALLEN AND SEBASTIAN HAVE WORKED SO HARD ON THIS SHOW.

THAT'S TRUE. THEY HAVE.
IT WOULD BREAK THEIR POOR HEARTS TO GIVE UP NOW.
WE COULD ALL BE FAMOUS! DON'T YOU GUYS WANT THAT?

UM...
WELL...

I THINK WHAT WE ARE TRYING TO SAY IS... NO. NOT REALLY.
BESIDES, CLAIRE, YOU AND GEORGIANA ARE GETTING ALL OF THE ATTENTION.

OH. OKAY, I DON'T WANT TO BE SELFISH OR PRESSURE YOU GUYS INTO SOMETHING YOU DON'T WANT.
BUT YOU'RE RIGHT. WE'VE GONE THIS FAR WITH IT. MAYBE WE SHOULD SEE IT THROUGH. BESIDES, LOOK ON THE BRIGHT SIDE, IT COULD STILL BE A MISERABLE FAILURE.

HERE THEY COME.

WE'RE HERE! AND WE BROUGHT YUMMY CHAI LATTES!

SOON...
GUESS WE WERE WORRIED OVER NOTHING. IT'S LIKE WE'RE NOT EVEN HERE.
BLAHBLAH. BLAH. BLAH BLAH, BLAH.

THE WEEKEND WEARS ON... AND ON...
HEY, GUYS MOM MADE SOME DINNER.

SO, THIS IS IT. THE FASHION SHOW IS THIS WEEK. WILL EVERYTHING BE DONE?
WE'RE ALMOST THERE. IF WE ONLY HAD ONE MORE WEEK.

IF ONLY SOME PEOPLE WEREN'T GETTING IN OUR WAY.
ME? YOU MEAN ME?

THAT'S NOT FAIR AND YOU **KNOW** IT!
OH, YOU **WOULD** SAY THAT! WHY DON'T YOU KEEP QUIET FOR A **CHANGE.**
HEY, GUYS. WE'RE ALL JUST TIRED.

KALLEN, MAY I SPEAK WITH YOU **OUTSIDE?**

WHAT IS YOUR **MALFUNCTION?**
DON'T GIVE ME **THAT.** YOU'VE BEEN ACTING LIKE A SELF-INVOLVED **DIVA** ALL WEEKEND!

OUR SHOW'S VIEW NUMBERS ARE **WAY** UP AND RISING. YOU HAVE **NO** IDEA WHAT IT TAKES TO MAKE A **HIT!**
A HIT? DON'T MAKE ME LAUGH. YOU THINK YOU'RE **FAMOUS?**

AT LEAST I'M ON MY WAY. AND YOU'RE **NOT** GOING TO **STOP** ME!
YOU-- OH, NOT **THIS** TIME!

DID I JUST SEE THAT? KALLEN IS A-- A-- WHAT IS HE? A FOX? THAT'S SO FREAKY.

ACTUALLY, IT'S A LITTLE BIT SEXY. BUT STILL... WOW. AND KAYA, TOO?

NO WONDER KAYA HAS BEEN SO UPSET ABOUT KALLEN'S SHOW. THEY'VE GOT A BIG SECRET TO HIDE.

WHERE ARE KALLEN AND KAYA?
UH... THEY MUST HAVE LEFT.

ZE FASHION SHOW TONIGHT HAS ZE HIGHEST ATTENDANCE IN ZE HISTORY OF ZE SCHOOL. IT'S WONDERFUL, BUT I CAN'T IMAGINE WHY.
L.A.H.S. OF FASHION & DESIGN
CALL FOR ENTRIES!
FALL FASHION SHOW
SOLD OUT
WHO KNOWS WHY THESE THINGS HAPPEN, MRS. BARTEAU.
CULTURAL TRENDS, MAYBE.

ONE CULTURAL TREND IN PARTICULAR.
DO YOU THINK NONE OF THE TEACHERS KNOW ABOUT IT YET?

HOW COULD THAT BE? IT'S THE BIGGEST THING IN SCHOOL!
MAYBE THEY DON'T SPEND MUCH TIME ONLINE. WHO KNOWS.

KAYA REYNARD, PLEASE COME TO THE OFFICE.
UH-OH. I THINK MAYBE SOMEBODY KNOWS.

WELL, SO MUCH FOR KALLENATION. THEY SAID KALLEN AND SEBASTIAN AREN'T ALLOWED TO FILM THE FASHION SHOW SINCE THEY DON'T HAVE MODEL RELEASES AND PERMITS.

BUT WE'VE FILMED ALL OF THE BUILDUP TO THIS SHOW. IT'S THE CLIMAX OF THE STORYLINE! IT'S ESSENTIAL.
YEAH, BUT THERE'S NO WAY. THEY AREN'T GOING TO LET YOU FILM. THEY'RE NOT EVEN GOING TO LET YOU IN.

WE'LL JUST SEE ABOUT THAT.
SEBASTIAN, ARE YOU READY FOR THE LIVE FEED ONCE I SET THE WEB CAM UP?
YEP!

SO, AS SOON AS I TURN IT ON WE'LL BE STREAMING LIVE ON OUR YOOSCREEN CHANNEL, RIGHT?

KAYA, I WANT TO WEAR THAT DRESS. I'VE DECIDED THAT IT'S A BETTER COLOR FOR ME UNDER THE RUNWAY LIGHTS.
BUT THE ONE YOU HAVE ON IS FITTED FOR YOU!

YOUR HAIR ALWAYS SEEMS SLIGHTLY DAMP.
I SWIM A LOT.
DO YOU THINK THESE FLOWERS SIT RIGHT?
IT WILL BE FINE, CLAIRE. ALL THE CLOTHES ARE BEAUTIFUL.

LIKE WHAT? KAYA, YOU ALWAYS EXAGGERATE.
YOU'VE BEEN ACTING LIKE THIS EVER SINCE WE STARTED HIGH SCHOOL AND YOU GOT SO POPULAR!
I PEEKED OUT FRONT. THE ENTIRE AUDITORIUM IS PACKED. PEOPLE ARE EVEN STANDING IN THE BACK!

CLICK

Kallenation, Episode 28, Season Finale
VIDEO FEED - LIVE VIDEO FEED - LIVE VIDEO FEED - LIVE VIDEO FEED -
65,440 Viewers Connected

HOLD STILL. I JUST WANT TO MAKE SURE THIS DRAPES RIGHT.
NEXT UP ON THE RUNWAY ARE THE SOPHOMORE CLASS FASHIONS...
EEEEEEE
EEEEEEEK!

KALLEN?

IT'S *FUZZY!*
WE FOUND HIM!

YES... IT'S FUZZY!

WAIT'LL I
GET YOU HOME,
FUZZY!

NEXT UP ARE FIVE OUTFITS DESIGNED BY CLAIRE LEO
CLAIRE! ARE YOU READY?
YES! GO, GO YOU GUYS!

MODELLING CLAIRE'S FASHIONS ARE: GEORGIANA CHELSEA...
ASHLEY ARCHER...

SUE-NI MACDUFFIE
RUBY ZARA
AND KAYA REYNARD.

NEXT WEEK AT SCHOOL...
I CAN'T BELIEVE THE EMAIL I GOT FROM THAT DESIGNER IN MILAN. HE SAYS SO MANY NICE THINGS!
AND YOU DESERVE IT! YOU DID AN AWESOME JOB!
WE DID AN AWESOME JOB!
WHAT'S THE LATEST WITH KALLEN'S SHOW?
OH, HE'S VERY TRAGIC. WHEN ALL THE PEOPLE WATCHING THE LIVE BROADCAST SAW THAT FUZZY WAS A FOX AND NOT A DOG, THE ANIMAL RIGHTS PEOPLE GOT ALL UP IN ARMS.
SO MANY PEOPLE CRITICIZED AND THREATENED HIM FOR OWNING AN ILLEGAL EXOTIC ANIMAL THAT HE HAD TO CANCEL THE SHOW.
WHAT ABOUT HIS DREAMS OF STARDOM?.
WE ALL HAVE OUR DREAMS. WE JUST HAVE TO MAKE THEM COME TRUE.

Watch Out For PAPERCUTZ™

Welcome to the fun, fashionable, friend-filled first STARDOLL graphic novel by JayJay Jackson from Papercutz, the fine folks dedicated to publishing great graphic novels for all ages. I'm Editor-in-Chief Jim Salicrup, and I'm here to give you a little bit of background on JayJay Jackson. So I asked her to tell us a little bit about herself:

"I can't remember a time when I didn't want to be an artist. My cousin tells me that at the age of six I was already set on it. Even with precious little encouragement or help in the beginning I obsessively stuck to the path. I became an artist because I HAD to. I've had an eclectic career. I've been an illustrator, graphic designer, art director, painter, writer, editor, web designer, etc. In comics I've worked at Marvel, DC, Valiant, Defiant, Broadway Comics and more.

"The art style in STARDOLL is inspired by the beautiful art on the Stardoll site itself. I've tried to translate that vision into the sequential art form. The emphasis of the book is on fun and fashion with great stories at its heart, so it works for all ages and genders. I think it will surprise people! With STARDOLL I was lucky enough to have an almost blank slate as far as the characters and story goes. Fashion and all other forms of art are my biggest passion in life! The opportunity to do a book with fashion as a central theme is a dream come true. My goal has been to create principle characters who are complex, yearn to reach their goals and have interesting backgrounds and lives and also happen to be female.

"It's been a lot of fun creating the world of STARDOLL and the people in it, based on the rich imagery and fun fashions of the Stardoll site. I'm hooked on the Stardoll site! I go there and play all the time. But not when I'm supposed to be working! I promise!"

Along with JayJay, we're committed to creating fun, fabulous, and surprise-filled STARDOLL graphic novels. Coming up next, will be STARDOLL #2 "The Secret of the Star Jewel." But in the meantime we also want to introduce you to another fun group of girls—Julie, Lucie, and Alia—who are as passionate about dance, as Ashley, Claire, Kaya, Ruby, and Sue-Ni are about fashion. They all star in another Papercutz graphic novel series, DANCE CLASS by Beka and Crip, and on the following pages we present a sneak peek at DANCE CLASS #6 "A Merry Olde Christmas." Whether you enjoy STARDOLL, DANCE CLASS, or any of the many other Papercutz graphic novels available to you, we want you to know that we want to hear from you. Tell us what you love or what let you down. We want to know what you think, because ultimately we're doing it all for you!

Thanks,
Jim

JIM & JAYJAY, A FEW YEARS AGO!

STAY IN TOUCH!

EMAIL: salicrup@papercutz.com
WEB: www.papercutz.com
TWITTER: @papercutzgn
FACEBOOK: PAPERCUTZGRAPHICNOVELS
SNAIL MAIL: Papercutz, 160 Broadway, Suite 700, East Wing, New York, NY 10038

SPECIAL PREVIEW OF DANCE CLASS #6
"A MERRY OLDE CHRISTMAS"

THE NEXT DAY...
I CAN'T BELIEVE YOU DIDN'T CALL OR TEXT US LAST NIGHT, JULIE!

OUR FRIEND PRUNE-- THE SAME PRUNE WHO'S STUDYING DANCE AT LONDON'S ROYAL BALLET SCHOOL-- INVITED US OVER FOR CHRISTMAS BREAK?
YES! I EVEN BROUGHT THE LETTER SHE SENT ME TO SHOW IT TO YOU!

SHE SAYS THAT A LONDON THEATER WANTS TO STAGE A MUSICAL FOR CHRISTMAS WITH CHILDREN AND TEENS ONLY!
!

PRUNE PROPOSES WE ALL TRY OUT TOGETHER! THEY'RE HOLDING AUDITIONS THE FIRST DAY OF WINTER BREAK, WHICH IS IN LESS THAN A MONTH!

AND WE CAN STAY AT HER HOUSE-- HER DAD'S COOL WITH IT!

I CAN'T BELIEVE SHE THOUGHT OF US! DO YOU THINK WE HAVE A CHANCE OF GETTING PICKED?
FOR SURE!
?

BUT IT'LL BE HARD TO CONVINCE OUR PARENTS TO LET US GO TO LONDON!

ALL THREE OF YOU HAVE DETENTION ON WEDNESDAY! THAT'LL TEACH YOU TO GOOF OFF IN MY CLASS!
!
!

NOW IT'LL BE EVEN HARDER TO CONVINCE OUR PARENTS TO LET US GO TO LONDON!

DON'T MISS DANCE CLASS #6 "A MERRY OLDE CHRISTMAS" – COMING SOON!